Book 2

THE Top-Secret Diary of Celie Valentine

Secrets Out!

Julie Sternberg

illustrated by Johanna Wright

Boyds Mills Press   An Imprint of Highlights   Honesdale, Pennsylvania

Boyds Mills Press
An Imprint of Highlights
815 Church Street
Honesdale, Pennsylvania 18431
boydsmillspress.com

Printed in the United States of America

ISBN: 978-1-62091-777-0 (hc) · ISBN: 978-1-62979-891-2 (pb) ·
ISBN: 978-1-62979-434-1 (eBook)

Library of Congress Control Number: 2015904691
First paperback edition, 2018
The text of this book is set in Zemke Hand ITC Std.
The illustrations are done in pen and ink.
Book design by Robbin Gourley
10 9 8 7 6 5 4 3 2

For my sister, Deborah, who has always kept my secrets
—JS

For Georgia B. Sisco
—JW

JOURNAL

PUT THIS JOURNAL DOWN RIGHT **NOW.**

DO NOT TURN THE PAGE.
IT IS **PRIVATE**.

That definitely includes you, Josephine Rosalie Altman. You do NOT get to open this just because you're my big sister. If you do not put it right back where you found it and walk away, I will tell your whole grade that when you eat strawberries you get a rash on your tushy.

I AM **NOT** KIDDING, JO.
NO, I AM NOT.

Dearest spectacular Celie,

While your mother and I were out earlier, she mentioned that you had asked for a new journal, since you've already filled your last one. So we stopped on our way home from my doctor's visit and picked this out for you.

I should buy something for you every day! It never fails to lift my spirits. Like this:

Dark Spirits
Lifting to Light

I hope that you enjoy this journal. How nice that the moments you describe in here will be forever available to you in these pages.

All my love,
Granny

THIS DIARY BELONGS TO

Celie Valentine Altman

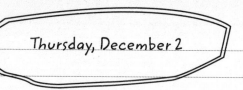

Thursday, December 2

I think I can stop being so worried about Granny's mind. I've been scared about it ever since she moved in a couple of weeks ago, because she keeps forgetting things. Like this morning, when she couldn't remember the word for eggs. And called them "oval things from chickens."

THAT definitely scared me. Since "eggs" is not a hard word.

But then I thought about it more. And I realized: Jo forgot her math notebook in a classroom after school today, which meant Mom and I had to wait FOREVER in the school lobby while she went back upstairs to find it. And no one's worried about Jo's mind.

Plus Mom forgot to give me my bag lunch a few weeks ago, when my class went to the Brooklyn Museum. She was holding it when we got to school, then she just left with it. Mrs. McElhaney had to buy me a lunch. It was embarrassing. But no one's worried about Mom's mind.

Also, Dad tells me all the time to stay calm when Jo annoys me. "Try reminding yourself, 'She's not an evil villain! She's just my big sister!'" But I never remember to do that. And my mind is fine.

So that's it. I am done worrying about Granny's mind. D-O-N-E, like when one of her sour-cream coffee cakes comes out of the oven, golden brown and cinnamon-y and delicious. Yum.

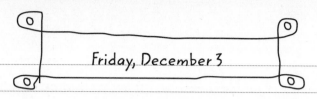

Friday, December 3

It turns out, Granny's a genius. Take for example the picture she drew in this journal, when she wrote her note to me. The picture of dark spirits lifting to light. It is very inspiring. I am inspired to draw my spirits so far today.

Here is a picture of my spirits ten minutes ago, when my best friend, Lula, called and asked me to come over tomorrow:

Light!

Dark

And here is a picture of my spirits five seconds later, when Lula said Violet was coming, too.

10

Why does Lula always have to invite both of us?
Violet never wants to do anything fun. Last time,
when we went to the movies, we didn't get a jumbo
popcorn with a giant box of chocolate-covered
raisins—the way Lula and I have for years and
years and years—because Violet said her stomach
wouldn't feel right afterward. Which made Lula
say, "Yeah, mine too, probably." So we just got the
popcorn. But stomachs are not the point! The point
is friendship tradition!

That movie did not feel as good without chocolate-
covered raisins. And it was all Violet's fault.

A Little Later

Now Jo is acting CRAZY.

Before she went bonkers, I was having a perfectly nice time in the kitchen with Mom and Granny. Even though I don't like being in the kitchen as much as I used to. Because it's gotten very cluttered in there. Ever since Mom cleared out her home office so we could turn it into a bedroom for Granny.

At first Mom tried putting all her files in cabinets in our living room. But the cabinets stopped closing, they had so much jammed in them. So Mom's been putting more and more of her papers on the kitchen table. Plus she's keeping boxes of staples and paper clips and pencils and pens and an electric pencil sharpener on the kitchen counter. A couple of plastic pencil sharpeners, too. There are pencil shavings EVERYWHERE. They're probably getting in our food.

What are these unusual crinkly bits inside of me?

Yuck.

I liked it better when Jo was the only messy one.

Anyway. That's not the point. The point is, Granny, Mom, and I were having a nice time in the kitchen.

Granny's banana bread was in the oven. She was sitting at the kitchen table, sketching on her sketchpad, in a spot that wasn't taken over by Mom's stacks. Mom was making a salad for dinner. And I was eating red peppers as she sliced them.

Then Jo rushed in. Her eyes were big, and some hairs were flying away from her head, and her cheeks looked sweaty.

"My phone—it's not in my backpack!" she cried.

Mom turned to Jo. In a super-serious voice, she said, "You lost your phone?"

"That's very bad," I said to Jo. Because Mom and

Dad had specifically told her not to lose that phone when they gave it to her a few weeks ago, as a surprise.

I should've gotten the phone instead. Even though I'm two years younger. I obviously would've been better about following the rules.

"It'll be very expensive to replace," I reminded Jo. "You might not get another one." Then I turned to Mom and said, "Right?"

"I DIDN'T lose it—I know EXACTLY where it is," Jo said. Not even letting Mom answer. "I remember very clearly putting it on the top shelf in my locker, right on the edge, after I looked at it before I went to science."

"Why did you look at it before science?" I said. "You're not supposed to touch the phone during school. Mom and Dad said that."

Jo glared at me and said, "I'm not even talking to

you. I'm talking to MOM."

"Well, MOM will tell you that you're not supposed to touch your phone at school," I said.

Then I waited for Mom to tell Jo that. And get really mad. But instead she shook her head and closed her eyes and paused for a long time.

I could tell what she was doing. She was counting backward to keep calm.

I hate when she does that. It takes forever.

Finally she opened her eyes said, "Let's all just please focus on what to do about the lost phone."

"IT'S NOT LOST!" Jo shouted. Like a crazy person. "You never listen to me. I JUST told you—it's in my locker, on the edge of the shelf, I KNOW it is. But I need to go back to school now and get it. Please let me go back—I need my phone TONIGHT, I really, really need it."

"JO!" Mom said. FINALLY sounding angry. "You know how much is going on. You know it's not an easy time. PLEASE do not pick this moment to have a tantrum about a phone."

I glanced at Granny then. Because she's the reason it's not an easy time. We're all worried about what the doctors will say about her mind. But Granny was sketching, not listening.

"All you do on your phone is—" I started to say to Jo. But she interrupted and jabbed a finger at me and shouted, "Stop talking—just STOP! This has nothing to do with you!"

Actually, it had everything to do with me. Because if Mom took Jo back to school, dinner would be very late, and I would starve.

But I didn't get to say that. Because Granny called to me then.

"Celie," she said, "please come sit next to me." She

set a napkin on top of her sketchpad and pulled out one of the kitchen chairs for me.

I never say no to sitting next to Granny. So I went and sat and put my elbow on a file of Mom's labeled "Royalties."

Granny peeled an orange and shared it with me while Mom told Jo they couldn't go back for the phone tonight. "Maybe tomorrow," Mom said. "Assuming the school's open over the weekend. We'll have to call and check."

"Tomorrow will be too late!" Jo said.

"You spent years and years without a phone," Mom said. "I think you can make it one more night."

"YOU DON'T UNDERSTAND!" Jo shouted. "NOBODY IN THIS WHOLE FAMILY UNDERSTANDS!"

Then she ran past me and out the door.

I saw her face for one second as she did, and it looked like she might have started crying. I thought about going to see if she actually had.

But then I got distracted by Granny's sketchpad. She'd put a napkin on top of it, but I could still see the edges of her picture. The one she'd been drawing while she sat at the kitchen table. And those edges got me worried.

"Is that—" I started to ask Granny. Then I didn't know how to finish my question. So I started again and said, "What is that?"

"Oh!" Granny said, realizing what I was looking at. "Nothing but an old lady's scribbles. I'm throwing it right out."

She ripped the drawing out of her sketchpad then and threw it in the tall garbage can by the window.

"Okay," I said, acting like I didn't care. I didn't want her to know that she was scaring me.

For a while after that, I just sat at the table, trying to seem interested in Mom and Granny's conversation. Pretending I'd forgotten all about that sketch.

But really I was waiting for a chance to sneak to the trash can and take it out. Also, I was wishing I could keep Mom from dumping pepper seeds and cucumber peels and wet paper towels on top of it.

It was a massacre. And there was nothing I could do to stop it.

ACK! I'M DROWNING IN HERE!

I FINALLY snuck Granny's sketch out of the trash.
After Mom had left the kitchen to check on Jo,
and Granny had gone to her room to rest before
dinner.

It wasn't easy to get all the gunk off that sketch.
But I did my best. Now at least it's less disgusting.

Here it is:

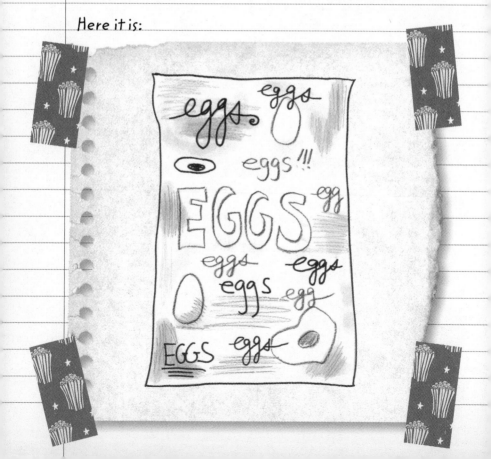

I don't want Granny to be thinking eggs, eggs, eggs, eggs, eggs, eggs. It makes me think maybe I DO need to be worried about her mind.

Except, maybe this is just Granny making a new kind of art?

But if that was it, wouldn't she just say so? Instead of throwing it out so fast?

I wish I could show the sketch to Jo and see what she thinks. Only, she locked herself in the bathroom and is refusing to come out. Even when I pounded on the door and told her I had to pee. She shouted from in there, "I NEED A PLACE TO MYSELF FOR ONCE! PLEASE, JUST LET ME HAVE A PLACE TO MYSELF!"

So I had to use Mom and Dad's bathroom.

I am NOT going to become a crazy person who locks herself in bathrooms when I'M in sixth grade. No, I am not.

I guess I could talk to Lula about both Granny and Jo tomorrow at her house. Since Lula is an understanding person and my very best friend. Except, Violet will be with us.

I am so sick of Violet being with us.

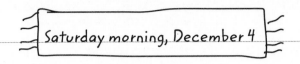
Saturday morning, December 4

I have nowhere to go in my own home. Except the HALL. Which is where I am, on the floor. Hoping nobody steps on me.

Our housekeeper, Delores, is dusting in my room, so I can't be in there. Dad's getting dressed in his room, Granny's getting dressed in hers, and the kitchen is a disaster. Crumbs and dirty dishes are EVERYWHERE. Plus Mom's working on Granny's insurance papers in the living room.

No one can go near Mom when she's working on insurance papers. They make her VERY CRANKY.

I can't even go in my own bathroom, because Jo's taking a shower. Her showers last FOREVER. I don't know why. She's a normal-sized person. There's not that much to wash.

She better not be using my conditioner. I love my conditioner. It smells like pomegranates.

A tiny Bit Later

I just went to tell Jo not to use my conditioner. The bathroom door was locked, so I pounded on it and shouted, "JO! OPEN THE DOOR! JO!"

Jo didn't even answer. But Mom did. She yelled from the living room, "STOP SHOUTING!"

And, before I could say a word, she yelled even louder, "I NEED QUIET!"

Dad stepped out of his room then.

"Shhh," he said, when he saw me. Then he pointed down the hall, in the direction of Mom, and whispered, "INSURANCE."

"I know, I know," I told him.

One second later, Jo FINALLY stepped out of the bathroom, wrapped in a big towel. AND SHE SMELLED LIKE POMEGRANATES!

I couldn't even yell at her! Dad was STILL standing there. I'd JUST told him I'd be quiet.

So I said to Jo, VERY calmly and VERY quietly, "You are not allowed to use my conditioner. Never, never, never. Not allowed." I sounded like a teacher, talking to a kindergartener.

"Nice work," my dad said. He seemed very proud.

But Jo looked at me like I was a lunatic. "Okey dokey, artichokey," she said. Then she went off to our room to get dressed.

I glared at Dad.

"That did not work," I told him. "She definitely did not listen."

"I have an idea," he said.

Then we hid the bottle of conditioner together, behind a big stack of towels.

Later

After we hid the conditioner, Dad took me to Lula's.
Now I'm back, and it's official. I was right about
Violet. She ruined everything.

They were both in Lula's room when I got there. I
could hear the sound of their voices as I walked
down the hall toward them. I couldn't tell what
they were saying, though.

Then, the second I walked into Lula's room, they
both got VERY quiet. They were sitting near each
other on Lula's soft carpet, and they looked up at
me with worried faces. Like they did NOT want me
to know what they'd just been saying.

I wanted to go home then. Because it felt like they
must've been talking about me.

But Lula was looking so sad and worried. I had to
ask her, "What's wrong?"

She shook her head and said, "Nothing." Then she smiled at me and said, "Come sit with us."

So I sat beside her, on her rug. Right in our snapping spot, where we'd taught ourselves to snap when we were really little.

"Let's all do something," Lula said. "What should we do?"

"I know," Violet said. Looking only at Lula. "Let's play that game Gracie made up at your movie party. It made you laugh so hard, remember?"

That was a MEAN thing to say! Because I was practically the only girl in the whole grade who hadn't been invited to that movie party. Lula and I were in a fight back then. Violet MUST have remembered that. That fight was the only reason she and Lula started being friends.

I crossed my arms and glared at Violet, who kept looking at Lula, as if I wasn't even in the room. And

I started getting a stomachache, remembering how my best friend in the whole world had decided to have a party without me. And, apparently, had done a lot of laughing without me.

Remembering that party made Lula feel bad, too. I could tell, the second I glanced at her. She'd turned blotchy in the face and was biting the top of her thumb. Like she does when she feels guilty.

I didn't want her to be blotchy and thumb-biting. Since we're friends again.

So I said to Lula—NOT Violet—"What are the rules of the game?"

Lula stopped biting her thumb and said, "You just, you know—you say one sentence about a movie. Not a very obvious sentence. And then people guess what the movie is. Like, for example—"

She looked away and thought for a second.

Then she said, "An old farmer dances to cure his little sick animal."

"Babe," I said, smiling at her, and she smiled at me, and everything was definitely all right between us. Because she'd chosen our all-time favorite movie, which we've loved from the very bottoms of our hearts forever.

Maybe Vicious Violet didn't like it that everything was all right between Lula and me. Because after we'd all played just a couple more rounds of the movie game, Violet said to Lula, "Remember when we were at your party and Nora said just one word—"

"'BOYS!'" Lula said, laughing. "She said, 'BOYS!'"

"And then Isabel started jumping up and down, saying, 'I know what movie it is! I know it!'" Violet said.

"And she was so WRONG!" Lula practically

shouted. Then they both LAUGHED and LAUGHED. Making me feel left out AGAIN.

I had to interrupt all that laughing. So I asked Lula if we could play our favorite game on her new phone. (HER parents let HER have a phone. Why can't mine?)

Anyway. That phone game has a baby koala riding on the back of an armadillo, and Lula and I love playing it and singing its very catchy tune.

But Violet wouldn't let us play it this morning. Because she has to limit her time on electronics. She actually said, "If I play now, my mom won't let me watch my show tonight."

Lula nodded and set down the phone. But I wanted to say, "So don't watch your show."

I had a very bad thought, too. I thought, What about your DAD, Violet? Would your DAD let you watch your show?

Which was a mean thing to think! Because Violet's dad moved to Oklahoma over the summer and hasn't even come back to visit her yet. That's what Lula told me.

I was feeling guilty about that terrible, mean thought when Lula's mom called us to lunch. So I left the biggest BLT for Violet. Even though I know that Lula's mom's BLTs are delicious.

Only, THAT was a mistake. Because Violet took all the yummy, crispy bacon out and set it on the side of her plate. Since fried food isn't healthy.

That poor, abandoned bacon.

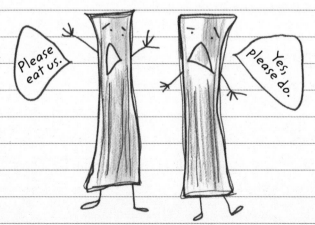

Later

I just made two pie charts about the fight Lula and I were having last month, when she didn't invite me to her party.

(We had to draw pie charts for math homework. So now I keep making pie charts in my brain.)

Here is my pie chart of what I thought at the BEGINNING of our fight:

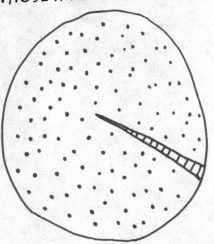

WHOSE FAULT IS THIS FIGHT?

 Lula

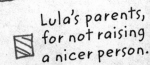 Lula's parents, for not raising a nicer person.

And here is my pie chart of what I thought by the very END of the fight:

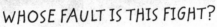

WHOSE FAULT IS THIS FIGHT?

I CAN'T TELL ANYMORE!

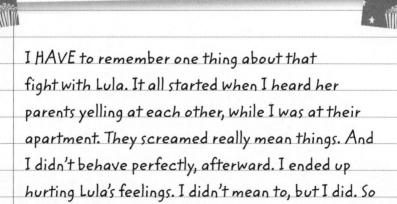

I HAVE to remember one thing about that fight with Lula. It all started when I heard her parents yelling at each other, while I was at their apartment. They screamed really mean things. And I didn't behave perfectly, afterward. I ended up hurting Lula's feelings. I didn't mean to, but I did. So

I have to be REALLY CAREFUL if anything like that ever happens again.

Luckily I haven't had to worry about it lately. Because I've only seen Lula's mom. Not her dad.

It's funny that they're never together now. I wish I could ask Lula why. And whether they screamed at each other a lot before I heard them. And whether they've kept screaming. And how she's feeling about it.

But I can't ask any of that. Because the screaming is the exact subject that started all of our problems.

I'm glad my parents don't scream at each other. They definitely argue, but they don't yell things like, "I don't want to live with you anymore!" Which is basically what Lula's parents were doing.

Also, I'm glad I never have to worry about my dad moving to another state. Like Oklahoma.

I do wonder this, though: Where is he right now? I haven't seen him since I got home.

Later

Dad took Jo to school, to get her phone. That's where he was. She got lucky because the school was open for a volleyball tournament. And because Dad didn't make her Suffer the Consequences of breaking our cell phone rules. Which is what he should've done.

Anyway, they're back now. And I didn't want to be annoyed with Jo. I wanted to TALK to Jo, about Violet's behavior at Lula's. Because ever since Jo finally got rid of her evil former best friend, Trina, it's been nice talking to Jo about friend meanness. It's been helpful.

So I was happy when she came home and sat on her bed and said, "How was Lula's?"

"You will not believe what Violet did," I said. And

then I started to tell her the story.

She should've listened! She should've scooted to the edge of her bed and given me all her attention, like she usually does when we talk about friendships.

Instead, she picked up her stupid phone, which she'd set beside her on the bed. And she started flipping through screens.

"What are you DOING?" I asked her. Instead of finishing my story.

"Just checking for texts," she said, still looking down at her phone.

"There's no new text," I told her. "Your phone buzzes when you get a new text. Remember? I heard no buzzing."

She ignored that and set the phone down again and turned to me and finally said, "What were you talking about?"

Of course I was ready to yell at her for NOT LISTENING TO ME, EVER. But we both got distracted. Because right that second her phone did buzz. Which meant she'd gotten a text. And her whole face got excited.

She picked up her phone and read the text. Then she turned blushy and grinned.

"What?" I said. "Why are you looking that way?"

I don't think she even heard me. She kept looking at her phone. Then she covered her mouth and thought for a second. Then she typed for a while. She covered her mouth again as she read over what she'd written.

That's when I reached over and tried to grab her phone. Because I needed to know—what was making her blushy and mouth-covery? It was WEIRD.

"Stop it!" she said, moving farther from me and

holding her phone close to her heart. "You can't just grab my phone like that—get away from me!"

"WHO is texting you?" I said.

She tried to look very casual. Then she said, "Amber," and raised her eyebrows and tilted her head. Which is EXACTLY what she does when she's lying.

"I can tell when you're lying," I told her. "Besides, you don't act like that when you and Amber text."

She doesn't. She doesn't blush or cover her mouth or read her texts a million times before sending when she's texting with Amber.

"I don't know what you're talking about, and you don't either," Jo said.

She stood up and raised her eyebrows and tilted her head and said, "I have to go to the bathroom."

"You're lying again," I said.

"You don't know when I have to go to the bathroom and when I don't," she said.

Then she walked quickly out of our bedroom. Still holding her phone to her heart.

She'll leave it behind at some point. And then I'll get a look at those texts. I'll be as sneaky as a ninja warrior.

Ninja Warrior
Me

Later

I found Granny in her room a little later. I love her room. I helped decorate it. I used her white tablecloth with pretty blue flowers (which she'd given to me as a birthday present) to cover Mom's ugly desk. Like this:

And I hung this painting
of a crushed coffee cup
that Granny had made
for Mom:

So she could see her
fabulous art on her wall.

"Jo's being annoying,"
I told Granny.

She was sitting in the armchair in the corner of
her room, reading. She set her book down for me,
though. And she said, "Let's do an art project, just
the two of us. That'll be a nice distraction."

We went to the kitchen, where we're keeping art
supplies now, plus a gazillion other things. Granny
found pencils and paper for us and set them on the
table. Then she started digging and digging through
the drawer to the left of the stove.

After a while I asked what she was looking for. "A spoon," she said.

"We keep them in a different drawer," I said. And I got one for her.

It was weird, how she kept looking and looking through that one drawer, instead of moving on to other drawers.

I don't want to think about that.

Doodling instead

Anyway, Granny came up with a great project.

"Draw this spoon three different ways," she told me. "Let your imagination run free. I'll do the same, and we'll call our work 'Views of a Spoon.'"

Here's what I came up with:

Spoon, Ready for the Red Carpet

I never get to spear anything. Fork does it all the time! It's not fair.

Angry Spoon

Zzzzzz

Just a spoon, taking a snooze.

Granny gave me hers, too. It's so different from mine! She explained that she used different art styles—something about dots and points, and Picasso, and another style she couldn't remember the exact name of.

Views of a Spoon

It's so smart, that drawing. Plus her spoons don't upset me at all. Which is good, because after her last drawing I started avoiding eggs. And it would be a lot harder to avoid spoons. Especially when Granny makes her famous butternut squash soup.

Yum

Later

Incredible news! Jo is texting a BOY! And not just any boy. Violet's brother, JAKE!

I know this because Jo finally walked away from her phone. She left it on her bed when she went to grab an apple. Good thing she uses the same password as on her computer.

She must have a crush on Jake. THAT'S why she got so blushy and grinny when she read that text earlier. I can't believe she likes HIM. He's a hundred feet

tall. And also, Violet told me and Lula that he bit
her in the stomach once. They were both very little,
but still! He's like Dracula.
A very tall Dracula.

At least Jake's in
the same grade
as Jo. Instead of
tenth grade, like the
last boy she had a crush on.
But does it have to be VIOLET'S
brother? Does Violet know? Does
she think Jo is RIDICULOUS? All
giggly and blushy? Is she talking to
Lula about it? Is THAT why they
got so quiet when I walked into
Lula's room the other day? Because
they were gossiping
about my sister?

I don't want anyone gossiping
about my sister. ESPECIALLY
not Violet.

Why does she have to be ALL OVER MY WHOLE LIFE now?

Anyway. I couldn't read the whole chain of texts
between Jo and Jake. Because it was long! And Jo
was only going to get an apple. I had to be fast!

Here's what I remember seeing:

WHAT IS HAPPENING ON WEDNESDAY? Jo
goes to rehearsals for her play right after school
on Wednesdays, and every other school day.
Rehearsals are AT SCHOOL and FREE. And if Jake
is paying, doesn't that mean this is a DATE?

She should've asked Mom or Dad for permission,
instead of saying "yes" right away, with a smiley
face! I have to ask
for permission before
I do anything. I can't
even go stand on the
sidewalk right outside
our building with
Lula, who I've known
FOREVER, without
getting permission. So
OBVIOUSLY Jo needs
permission to skip
rehearsal and go on a
DATE with
a strange boy!

You're too young to date, Missy!

I'm going to find a school calendar. To see if there's a school-sponsored activity that costs money on Wednesday afternoon.

The tiniest bit later

The calendar was on the kitchen counter, under Mom's office supply collection. Paper clips spilled everywhere when I pulled the calendar out.

Those things take forever to clean up.

Anyway. I looked in the calendar. There is
NOTHING going on after-school on Wednesday.
Except for an afterschool class in knitting. I don't
know whether it costs money. But I am certain
Count Jake-ula is not taking Jo to that.

I vahnt
to knit
and sew.

So, where exactly are the two of them going?

Later

I just looked through our bookshelves until I found the school yearbook from last year. Because I couldn't remember exactly what Jake looks like. Here's a picture of that tall boy:

And here's the horrifying picture I cannot get out of my mind:

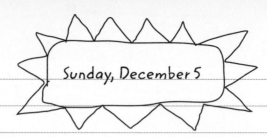

Sunday, December 5

I just did something weird. I hid under Jo's bed while she was out of our room. Because I figured she'd come back in and probably call Amber and tell her about Jake and Wednesday. I wanted to spy on her while she did.

Here is my spy report:

From the
Top-Secret Spy Notebook of
Celie Valentine Altman

A spy disguises all aspects of his or her appearance. When you speak to your target, trying using a much deeper voice than usual.

I'm pretty sure Jo knows me even when I talk in a deep voice.

Besides, I'm not going to speak to my target. I'm HIDING from my target.

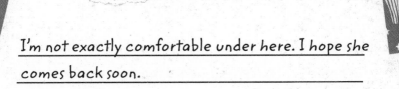

I'm not exactly comfortable under here. I hope she comes back soon.

Try wearing perfume to disguise your scent.

I have a scent? I don't want a scent.

Besides, I don't own perfume. Am I supposed to steal some?

And also, has anyone ever cleaned under here? There are a LOT of dust bunnies.

Clothes are another important tool for altering appearance. Consider wearing one vividly colored item, such as a red scarf, as a distraction.

My hands and arms are covered in grime. I bet my jeans are, too, but I can't see them. I'm lying on my stomach. I want to take a bath. Yuck.

Wait—I hear something.

I had to stop writing in my notebook then. Because
Jo came in. I guess she heard me writing. Or
maybe fidgeting around, trying to get comfortable.
Because she looked right under her bed and said,
"What are you DOING under there?"

Then she saw my spy notebook. And she said,
"Were you about to spy on me?"

"No, definitely not," I said. But she's my sister, and
she knew I was lying, and she said, "I gave you that
spy notebook as a gift! You're never allowed to use it
on ME—that should be obvious!"

So I said, "FINE." I crawled out, and I was covered
with dusty filthiness. Plus I still don't know anything
about Wednesday.

It was not a successful spy moment.

I don't think a red scarf would've helped.

I keep feeling dirty in my own house. I don't like it. I made these pie charts about it:

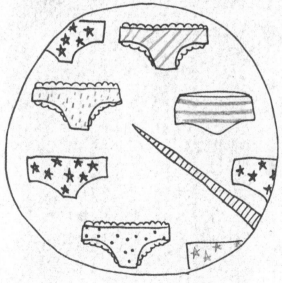

WHO MADE THE MESS IN OUR HOUSE <u>BEFORE</u> GRANNY MOVED IN?

 Jo, leaving her underwear on MY BED, and much, much more

 the rest of us

WHO MAKES THE MESS IN OUR HOUSE <u>NOW</u>?

Jo, still messy

Mom and Dad,
getting worse and worse

I don't blame Mom and Dad for the dirt under Jo's bed, though. Just Jo. How did she get it so grimy under there? There aren't nearly as many dust bunnies under my bed. I just checked.

I have been paying close attention to Jo today. Here
is what she has done: She's asked Mom to quiz her
on her Spanish vocab, and she's watched a little
football with Mom and Dad, and she's helped them
make dinner. (Because it is
her turn for that chore.)

Here is what Jo has NOT
done: She has NOT had a
private conversation with
either Mom or Dad. Which
means she has NOT told
either one of them that
she is skipping rehearsal
in three days and going on
her very first date, with a
giant who has a history of
sister-biting.

What should I do
about this?

Hmm

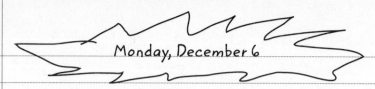

Monday, December 6

Math was miserable today. Because Lula and Violet
kept passing notes, back and forth and back and
forth. Right in front of me.

I wish their desks were behind mine, so I wouldn't
have to see.

I could tell something was bothering Lula, too.
Because she kept twisting her hair while she waited
for Violet to pass a note back on that sheet of
paper that they kept folding and unfolding.

If Lula is twisting her hair, something is definitely
bothering her.

I kept thinking, Why isn't Lula writing ME when she's
upset? Why VIOLET?

I couldn't think of a single good reason.

Finally, the bell rang. I didn't get up like everybody
else. I sat and tried to decide what to say to

Lula. But she and Violet moved so fast! In FIVE SECONDS, they were whispering together and walking out of class together.

They passed me on their way to the door at the back of the room. And they paid no attention to me at all.

When they were right beside me, I saw something sticking out of Violet's back pocket. A folded piece of paper covered with writing.

I knew what that paper was. And it was SO CLOSE to me.

I reached out fast and grabbed it.

Then I sat on it, and I froze. Waiting to get yelled at.

But nobody'd noticed! I guess Violet didn't even feel that folded paper leave her pocket. She and Lula just kept whispering and walking out the door. Everyone else kept walking, too.

Finally, when I felt very safe, I shoved the paper in
my backpack. And didn't take it out until I'd locked
myself alone in my room. Right here, on my bed.
And now I can't even believe what I just read.

Lula's dad is moving out! Her parents must be
getting a divorce. It's HORRIBLE.

Here's the whole conversation:

V—Dad found a place he likes!
Already! He's taking me
to see it tonight. -L

But he said it would take weeks!

I know! And he said he'd find something
close! It's not even walking distance. We
have to take the subway 4 stops.

At least he's already taking you to see it.
And you don't need a plane.

I can't _believe_ you still haven't seen your dad's place. Only a few more weeks!

I'm kind of scared to go now. It's weird. He's my dad. But you don't have to be scared. You'll see yours all the time.

At least you got a new sister!

A stepsister. Who won't say my name. She calls me "Geranium" if she answers the phone when I call Dad.

She'll change once she meets you. I know it. She'll love you! I always wanted a sister.

She'd just call you Lo_la. Or something strange, like Ballpoint Pen. You're actually very lucky.

I feel _unlucky_. But thanks for trying, Sky High Vi.

I feel so many things, reading this note! I feel
terrible that Lula's parents are separating. That
must be so hard for her. Knowing they're not going
to be a family anymore. Having to go down into the
subway and then wait four stops and come up in
a strange neighborhood, just to see her dad. Not
being able to wake him up in the middle of the
night and ask him to get her some water.

Also, I don't understand why she didn't tell me!
I've known her family forever! I know how weird
it's going to be for her. Not Violet. Even if Violet's
parents are divorced. Violet's only really been
friends with Lula since last month!

I can't believe I can't even talk to Lula about any of
this! I have to pretend everything's normal. I don't
know how long I can do that! What if I mess up?

And the whole time Lula will still be talking to
"SKY HIGH VI." When did they start using THAT
nickname?

"Geranium" is funnier. But still, Violet's stepsister shouldn't be using it. She should be nicer to Violet right now. Since they haven't even met yet, and they're at the start of being in the same family. It doesn't seem right.

Also, how does Violet already HAVE a stepsister? Her dad just moved away over the summer. People don't usually get stepsisters that fast. It seems weird.

I wonder if Lula's dad will ever marry someone else. I guess Lula might not even tell me if he does. I guess I might not ever see his new apartment, either.

I wish she'd at least give me a secret nickname. Even a ridiculous one, like Sky High Vi. Why couldn't I be Deep Sea Celie?

Deep Sea Me

It's not okay that Violet's parents are divorced.
It gives her an unfair friendship advantage.

Later

I don't have space in my brain and heart to think
about Lula and Violet anymore. Because of what
just happened.

I was walking down the hall, and I passed Granny's
room. She was sitting in a chair, holding one of
her shoes. A shoe she wears all the time. And she
looked so confused.

I stopped and said, "Granny? Is something wrong?"

She didn't reply. She just kept looking at the shoe.

Dad came up behind me then.

"How are you, Granny?" he said.

She looked up and held the shoe out to him and

said, "What is this? What do I do with it?"

I wanted to help. And I guess I wanted the situation to not feel serious. So I said to Granny, "It's your shoe, Silly Rabbit."

Dad said, "Celie—shhh," and put his hand on my shoulder. So I realized that I'd said something wrong. It must have seemed like I was calling Granny dumb. Which I never meant to do!

I wished I could grab that Rabbit sentence and put it back in my mouth.

I started trying to make things right. I said, "I just meant—I was just thinking that you love that shoe, Granny. You had it on today."

Granny looked at the shoe with her forehead scrunched, like she was trying so hard to understand. Then her whole face mushed up, and she started to cry.

"Oh, no!" I said. "No, no, no! Don't cry!"

That's when Dad said, "You go put on your pajamas, Celie. I'll take care of Granny."

"I don't want to go!" I said. I couldn't possibly go! I'd made Granny cry!

But Dad said in a very serious voice, "I need to tend to Granny. It's important that you go ahead. I'll be there in a minute."

So I went ahead, and I put on my pajamas. Then I sat down on my bed. And I started to cry.

I was alone for a while.

I drew this picture.

Then Dad and Mom and Jo came in.

"Please just tell me WHY we're meeting," Jo said, as Dad shut the door.

Then she took a look at me and said, "What's the matter?"

"Give your father a minute to explain," Mom said.

"I made Granny cry!" I told Jo.

"No, Celie," Dad said. "She was upset with herself, not with you."

"There's no way you made Granny cry," Jo told me. "No way. Anybody who knows you could tell you that."

I started crying harder then. Jo sat beside me and put her arm around me and said, "Just let Dad tell us. I know you didn't do anything bad to Granny."

Dad told the whole story of what had happened. "Granny cried because she knows she's not understanding what she should," he told me. "Not because of anything you did."

I shrugged. I didn't want her to cry because of me, and I didn't want her to cry because she was losing her understanding, either. Plus I wanted her to keep her understanding.

Then Dad said to me and Jo, "I'm so sorry this is happening."

"Granny is going to have good times and bad times," Mom said. "There might be more and more bad times. But there will be good times, too."

"Is that what the doctors are saying?" Jo said.

"Yes," Mom said.

"We'll take care of her through all her bad times, right?" I said. "She'll stay right here with us?"

"I think so," Mom said. "I hope so."

"You have to KNOW so," I said. A tear was dripping off my chin. I wiped it, and my cheeks, with the back of my hand.

"I wish I could," Mom said. "But so much is uncertain. I don't want to make false promises."

"Things would have to get very, very bad for Granny to have to leave," Dad said. "And then she would go to a place that specializes in caring for people just like her. But we're not there yet."

"I wish this weren't so hard," Mom said. "I never want things to be hard for you."

She started sniffing then, and Dad lowered his head. And I hated that we were all sad, and I hated why. So I said, "She's not DEAD."

"Right!" Dad said, looking at me. "She is absolutely not. Not even close."

"She's mostly GOOD," Mom said. "Maybe you'll bake with her tomorrow after school, Celie. She'd love that."

"I'd love it more," I said.

Then I went into the kitchen to write up a grocery list. So Mom could shop for ingredients while I was at school.

I decided we should make the most complicated recipe I could find in Granny's cookbook. So we would have lots of time together. I chose a twelve-layer cake. It should take FOREVER.

Oh boy, am I hard to bake!

Later

Everyone else is asleep but me.

I can't stop thinking.

I was so tired this morning. And it felt different, looking at Granny across the table from me at breakfast. I felt sorry for her. Because she doesn't know how to use shoes anymore.

I HATED feeling sorry for her. I just wanted to love her.

I had to change feelings. So I looked at Jo, and I said, "What are you doing today after school?"

"Going to play rehearsal with Amber," she said.

"And tomorrow?" I said. "WEDNESDAY. What are you doing after school on Wednesday?"

She looked at me a little funny and said, "Going to rehearsal with Amber. Just like every other weekday for the past three weeks."

"Really?" I said. "Right after school on Wednesday

you're going to rehearsal with Amber?"

"What are you DOING?" she said.

"What are YOU doing?" I said.

She glared at me, and I glared at her, and Dad said,
"Am I missing something?"

Then Granny said, "Would you please pass the salt?"

Which was a very sad thing to ask. Because she was
eating cereal, and she was pointing at the sugar.

I passed her the sugar instead of the salt. And I
felt angrier at Jo than I'd ever felt in my whole life.
Even though I knew Granny's mind wasn't Jo's fault. I
didn't care.

After breakfast Jo followed me out of the kitchen
and into our room. She closed the door behind us
and opened her eyes very wide and said, "I cannot
BELIEVE you read my texts."

"I cannot believe you're going on a DATE and you're not telling Mom and Dad," I said.

"It's not a DATE," she said. "We're just getting ice cream two blocks from school and walking right back. Then I really am going to rehearsal with Amber."

"You can't be late for rehearsal," I said.

"You don't know anything about anything," Jo said. "And I'm changing the password to my phone RIGHT NOW."

"FINE," I said. "But you HAVE to tell Mom and Dad about the date. Or I will. We have enough troubles in our family right now. You shouldn't be lying about going places with boys."

"You are so embarrassing!" she said. Which made no sense.

"Promise me," I said. "Promise you'll tell Mom and Dad."

"Fine," she said. "I'll tell them tonight."

Then she picked up her phone and started jabbing at it. "Password officially changed," she said.

And that was the end of THAT loving conversation.

Later

I wasn't so nice to Lula, either, today. Because she'd hurt my feelings. Trusting Sky High and not me.

First I didn't say hi to either one of them when I saw them before the first bell rang. They were sitting on a bench together outside our classroom. I didn't stop and talk to them. I just passed them and walked into the classroom and sat at my desk.

Lula said hi to me when they came in. Violet did, too. I nodded. But I didn't say hi back.

And in science I didn't check to see whether they wanted to be my lab partners for our study of sponges living in the shallow edges of the ocean. I asked Nora to be my partner instead.

I feel bad that I stopped spending time with Nora, after Lula and I ended our big fight. It was wrong. She's still nice to me, though. She's a very nice person.

Anyway. Lula gave me a "What's going on? Why aren't you with us?" look, from her lab station. But I shrugged and turned away.

Now she'll probably never talk to me again. And Jo will probably never talk to me again. And I'll live in silence, like a sponge.

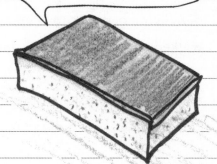

Even Later

I've been waiting and waiting for Granny to wake up from her nap. So we can bake together. But her doctor's appointments must have really wiped her out today. She's still sleeping.

Mom's been quieter than usual, too. I found her on the living room couch, with an old photo album on her lap.

I didn't have to ask what she was looking at. I knew. I sat down beside her.

She showed me pictures of Granny burping her when she was a little baby, and holding her hand when she was just learning to walk.

"This one's my favorite," she said. She pointed to a picture of Granny alone, standing in her Louisiana yard, shading her eyes and looking out.

"She was probably making sure I was staying out of

the street," Mom said. "I can hear her now, calling, 'Lizzie! Take three steps back from the curb!'"

I like that picture, too. I'm going to try to draw it here:

Maybe I'll paint it, too. In watercolors, for Granny.

Still the Same Bad Day

Jo interrupted my painting when she got home from rehearsal. She threw her stuff down near her bed and stomped back out of the room. Without saying a single word to me. Even though she obviously saw me at my desk.

So I yelled after her, "NOW is a good time to tell Mom! About you-know-what!"

She stomped back in and said, "FINE, since you're just going to tell her if I don't. But do not even think about spying on me while I do it."

"FINE," I said back. But then I wished I hadn't. Because I needed to hear that whole conversation. How else was I supposed to know what they both said?

I didn't spy, though. Since Jo was already so mad at me. Instead, when I heard Mom and Jo go into Mom's bedroom, I walked v-e-r-y s-l-o-w-l-y down the hall past Mom's room, on my way to the kitchen. For a banana. A healthy snack.

Luckily Mom hadn't closed her door all the way. So I heard this during my slow journey:

JO: "...back in time for my part of rehearsal."

MOM: "Be sure to stay with your friend the whole time, and be careful."

JO: (after a pause) "You don't care whether the friend is a girl or a boy, right?"

MOM: (after another pause—a longer one) "I guess that's right. As long as it's just ice cream and straight back for rehearsal."

I almost turned around then and barged in on that conversation. Because Jo wasn't describing it right! Jake isn't just a friend who's a boy! Mom needed to know that.

But I wasn't supposed to be listening, and I didn't
want to tell Mom that I'd read the Jo—Jake
texts without permission, and I also didn't want
Jo even MADDER at me. So I kept walking
to my banana.

Drop-off at school this morning was crazy! Because Sky High and Count Jake-ula were in the lobby with their mom when we got there. We ended up standing in a cluster near the front door, like this:

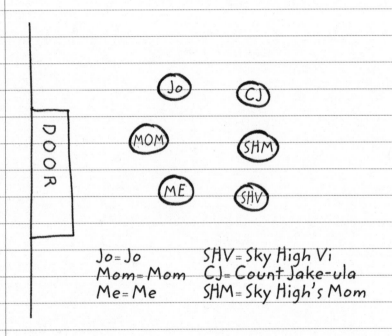

Jo = Jo
Mom = Mom
Me = Me
SHV = Sky High Vi
CJ = Count Jake-ula
SHM = Sky High's Mom

Violet said hi to me, and I said hi back. Then Jake nodded at Jo and said, "What's up?" And Jo turned pink and said, "Nothing much."

Mom took a look at Jo's face. Then she leaned toward Jo and whispered, too loudly, "Is that the boy—"

Super-fast, Jo hissed, "Shh!"

I knew then that Mom understood the whole Jo–Jake situation. Which was good.

Then I thought, Jake looks like a giraffe. Because he kind of leans over like one, when he's wearing a backpack.

See?

While I was watching Jake, Violet looked at me with

raised eyebrows. And I realized she definitely knew, too. About Jo and Jake.

Then I thought, OF COURSE she knows. Jake probably told her. Because EVERYONE tells Sky High Vi EVERYTHING. And I'D never know ANYTHING if I didn't spy and steal.

Then I got very distracted. Because Lula came into the lobby with her dad. They walked over to us and stood across from Jo. Like this:

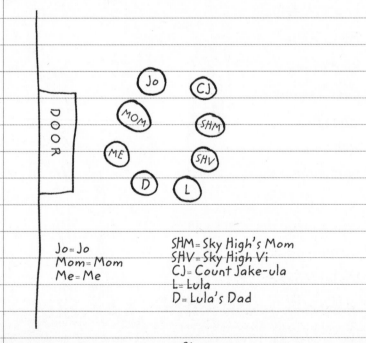

Jo= Jo
Mom= Mom
Me= Me

SHM= Sky High's Mom
SHV= Sky High Vi
CJ= Count Jake-ula
L= Lula
D= Lula's Dad

Right away my mom said to Lula's dad, "I haven't seen you in a while, Peter. How is everything?"

"Oh . . ." Lula's dad said. Then, after a long pause, he said. "You know." And then he paused AGAIN.

He was obviously waiting for my mom to say something. But she said nothing. Because she didn't know.

Finally, she started to say, "Um," just as Lula's dad was saying, "I'm sure Celie told you."

My mom gave me a confused look.

I shrugged and blushed. Because I shouldn't have known what Lula's dad meant, but I did. Then I glanced at Lula. She'd turned blotchy and taken a step away from her dad. And she was looking at the floor.

"No," my mom said slowly. "Celie and I have had so much going on at home, we haven't discussed it. I hope everything's okay."

"Well," Lula's dad said. "Jeannie and I—"

"DAD!" Lula cried. She was still looking at the floor.
"Just—stop talking."

"Oh," Lula's dad said. He sounded confused
and surprised. He smiled at my mom and said,
"My daughter wants me to stop talking."

My mom was looking from Lula to me. Obviously
wondering what Lula hadn't told me and why.

Jo was doing the exact same thing.

Jake looked like he had no idea what anyone was
talking about.

But VIOLET wasn't confused. VIOLET obviously
knew everything. She had her hand over her mouth,
and her eyes were wide, and she was looking at Lula,
and she was obviously thinking, "Uh-oh."

I hated that everyone was standing there wondering what was happening between me and Lula. Everyone except for VIOLET.

"I have to go to the bathroom," I said. Lula looked up then, and I gave her a "How could you not tell me?" look. And I left the lobby.

Lula hurried after me.

"I'm sorry I didn't say anything before," she said, when she caught up. "My parents are separating. My dad's moving out."

For a second I thought I should pretend to be shocked. But then I realized I didn't have to. And I said, "I figured something like that was happening, from the way your dad was just acting. I'm sorry they're separating."

"I feel bad that I didn't tell you," Lula said.

"Why didn't you?" I said. "I don't understand."

"I THOUGHT about telling you," she said. "I did. But—your family's too perfect."

"MY family?" I said. I thought of Granny and eggs and shoes, and Jo locking herself in bathrooms, and me screaming at Jo, and Jo screaming at me. "My family is DEFINITELY NOT perfect."

"Yes it IS, compared to mine," she said. "And right now it's easier for me to talk to someone who knows what this is like. Like Violet."

I did something VERY STUPID then. I shook my head and blurted out, "Sky High Vi." I wasn't thinking! I was upset! And SO SICK of Violet!

Lula looked at me hard and said, "What did you just say?"

"Nothing," I said quickly. And I bit my bottom lip.

"How do you know that name?" she said. "It's

secret." Then she thought for a second and said, "Wait—"

Her eyes grew wide and she put her hands on her hips. And she GLARED at me.

"You stole our notes!" she said. "I can't BELIEVE it. Violet said she thought you'd taken the paper from her pocket, and I DEFENDED you! I said you wouldn't do that."

"Um," I said. I couldn't think of anything else to say, but that didn't actually matter. Because Lula was talking fast and loud.

"Those were my private thoughts you stole!" she said. "And you just told me you figured it out from what my dad said. You already knew, from the notes! You lied. You can't steal and lie! It's not right."

Then she stomped away from me, down the hall.

I still can't believe it. I've lost Lula AGAIN. And this

time it's a hundred percent my fault.

WHOSE FAULT IS THIS FIGHT?

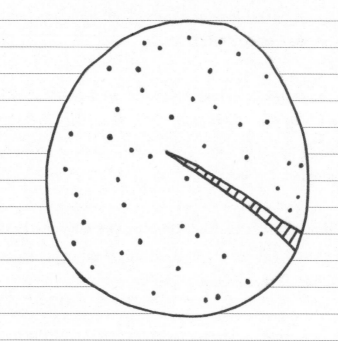

 Celie Valentine Altman   Violet's Stupid Nickname

I tried to apologize to Lula later, in math. I sat in my desk behind her and Violet, and I wrote this note:

L—I'm sorry! Do you want me to write down a
bunch of private thoughts and fold them up and
put them in my back pocket for you to steal?
I'm so so so so sorry. —C

I leaned far forward and put that note on Lula's
desk. But she didn't open it. She just turned and
stuck it back on my desk.

Then she started passing notes to VIOLET again.

I don't know what those notes actually said. I
couldn't have stolen them even if I'd wanted to
(which I DIDN'T). Because Lula ripped them into
tiny pieces at the end of the class and dropped
every single little piece into her backpack.

Here is what I'm afraid they said:

Dear Sky High,
You were right and I was wrong. Celie IS a terrible
person. I can't believe I was friends with her for

all those years. You're a much better friend. Want
to spend every day of every weekend together for
the rest of our lives, and talk about all the things
we have in common and make up really great
nicknames for each other? And never, ever include
Celie?

xo,
Lula

Dear Lula,
Sure! As long as we don't eat any candy or French
fries or brownies or bacon. Actually, anything
remotely tasty. Or stay on your phone for more
than five seconds. And the five seconds need to be
educational.

Lots of love,
Violet

So Lula and Violet will spend all their free time
together from now on, and Jo will be with Jake, and
when any of them see me they'll do this:

No one is ever going to like me again.

Later

This is now officially the worst day of my life. And it isn't even because of Lula.

At first the afternoon wasn't so bad. Dad was at work and Jo had her date plans, so it was me and Mom and Granny. Mom noticed that I was feeling sad and she tried to help. She kept asking questions like, "Are you okay?" And, "Are you sure you're okay?" And, "Is there anything you'd like to talk about?"

I just said, "No, thanks." And, "I'm fine." Because I didn't want to tell her that I'm a thief and a liar.

Eventually Mom had to go run some errands. As she was walking out the door, she said, "Why don't you and Granny bake? I bet you'd both love that."

Granny and I decided that was a great idea. Especially because we were supposed to bake yesterday, only Granny kept napping.

And, at first, it was great. Granny and I both put on aprons. I would've gotten the recipe for the twelve-layer cake, but Granny said, "How about brownies? My mother and I used to bake brownies together. She always wore a blue apron with pockets and a ruffle." Which was such good remembering! Plus I love brownies. So I said, "That sounds perfect."

And then Granny had a genius moment. We were

doubling the recipe, and I forgot to double the vanilla, and she corrected me!

"It's important to have enough vanilla," she said. "In fact, I like to throw in a little extra." And she added a splash of extra vanilla.

So I wasn't just baking with Granny. I was LEARNING from Granny.

Only, something bad happened about one minute later. Because about one minute later, Granny said, "Did we put in the vanilla? It's important to have enough. Actually, I like to throw in a little extra." And she started to add MORE vanilla.

I had to stop her and say, "Yes, Granny—we already put in extra."

"Oh," she said. She set the vanilla down and smiled at me a little. "Sorry."

"That's okay," I told her.

97

And everything WOULD have been okay, if that had been all. But it wasn't.

After we'd put the brownies in the oven to bake, Granny said, "Now we turn up the heat." Only, we didn't need to turn up the heat. Because the oven was at the exact right temperature. And also, she was reaching for the wrong knob. She was reaching for a STOVE knob—which shoots up flames.

I tried to stop her. I said, "No, Granny—wait." But she was already turning on the stove.

Flames started jumping out of one of the burners, and she didn't move back—she just stood there for a second, and the sleeve of her striped sweater was drooping, and the flames kept reaching, and that sleeve caught on FIRE! There were actual flames coming up from her sweater!

I shouted at her to get back, and I turned off the stove, and without even knowing what I was doing I grabbed the kettle that Mom keeps for tea on another part of the stove and I poured cold water from the kettle up and down Granny's arm.

Thank goodness there was water in the kettle.

The fire went out, which was good. And it didn't get to Granny's skin—I checked her arm. Only her sweater was burned. Which was very good.

But she kept saying things like, "What are you doing? You're watering me. I'm wet." And then, finally, she looked at me and said, "Did I do something wrong?"

"No, Granny," I said. "You didn't do anything wrong." That wasn't a lie, either. Because she didn't understand what she was doing when she set her sweater on fire. So she was CONFUSED. Not wrong.

She got calm then. And I could only think of one thing—I had to get rid of her sweater. Because if Mom or Dad realizes Granny is starting fires, they might not let her stay. They'll probably send her away.

I dried her arm gently with a dish towel and convinced her to take off her sweater and hand it to me.

"I will give it to you, if you want it," she said.

I feel so sad now, thinking about her saying that. Because it's always been true. I can't think of anything she's ever not given me. If I wanted it.

I miss my old Granny. I do. I miss her.

But that's not the end of what happened.

I took the burned striped sweater from her and got her to go sit in the living room. Because I can't leave her alone in the kitchen anymore.

"I have to do something very fast," I told her. "I'll be RIGHT back. Please wait there for me."

Then I RAN out of our apartment into the hallway, and I opened the chute that sends trash down to the basement. I threw the sweater down the chute and let the door to the chute bang shut.

The elevator dinged then, and I spun around, and Jo stepped off it, into the hallway. I blocked her view of the chute, even though she couldn't possibly have seen the sweater. The door to the chute was shut, and the sweater had slid down.

It turned out, all she needed to see was my face.

"What is it—what happened?" she said.

She looked so worried, and I was so worried, and the situation was so terrible. I started crying, and I told her the story as fast as I could. She had to ask me to repeat some parts. Because my voice was shaky and I didn't want to speak too loud.

"You can't tell Mom and Dad—you CAN'T," I told her, when I'd finished. I was wiping tears and runny nose off my face.

"I know, I get it, I won't," she said. She dug through her backpack and handed me a piece of crumpled paper. "For the guck on your hands," she said.

I cleaned my hands for a second with the paper. Then we hurried inside. To take care of Granny.

Later

Dinner was bad from the very beginning. Because I worried every second about what Granny would say. Jo did, too. I could tell, because we kept glancing at each other.

The first scary moment came when Dad said, "How was everybody's day?"

"Fine," I said, very fast. And Jo said, "Fine," very fast, too. Then we both looked with worried faces at Granny. I held my breath and hoped she wouldn't say, "I set myself on fire. Right, Celie? We did that together."

Luckily, she did not say that. She didn't say anything at all. She just smiled at Dad and ate some turkey meatball. So I let out my breath.

But then Mom said, "And how was the baking, Celie and Granny?"

Before Granny could say a word, I tried hard to change the subject. I said, "You know what it reminded me of? It reminded me of that time we baked lemon squares in Louisiana and that friend of Granny's came over, and she ate FOUR lemon bars and said they were the best she ever had. Remember that, Granny?"

Granny stopped eating for a minute, and we all watched her and waited for her to answer. Then waited some more. Finally, she said, "I miss Mama's fern." And she sounded so sad.

It was definitely a weird answer. And I was sorry about the sadness in her voice. But at least she didn't say she'd set herself on fire.

Mom and Granny talked about that fern for a while. I remember it. Granny always loved showing it to us when we visited her in Louisiana. It belonged to her mom first, before she died. It's survived miraculously, for years and years and years. It looks like this:

Anyway, I relaxed as they talked about the fern. I thought we'd make it through the dinner safely. But then, all of a sudden, Granny turned to Mom and said, "I gave Celie my striped sweater today."

My heart started jumping then, and my hands started sweating. I glanced at Jo. She'd sat up very straight. Like she was getting ready to push back her chair and stand and make an announcement.

"How nice," Mom said to Granny. "I know how much you love that sweater."

"We might need to fix it for her," Granny said.

That's when my heart dropped to the ground and splattered.

"What do you mean?" Mom asked Granny. "What happened to it?"

Granny drummed her fingers on her mouth a little. We were all so quiet, and I stopped breathing. Until finally Granny gave us a little smile that looked like an apology. And she said, "My memory's not so good these days."

I have to admit something very bad now. In that

moment—ONLY that moment—I was glad Granny's mind is not working so well.

But my problems were not all solved. Because Mom turned to me and said, "Is there something wrong with the striped sweater?"

And all I could think of to say was, "Uhhh." Because Mom HATES when I lie to her. And I couldn't tell her the truth.

Then Jo was a genius. She started talking, fast, about a grammar test she has tomorrow. "I'm not sure how to study—I'm really worried about it," she said.

Nothing distracts Mom and Dad more than schoolwork that we're really worried about. Plus Mom is obsessed with grammar. They talked about that test for the whole rest of the meal. So I was saved.

Except, what am I going to do if Mom ever asks to see the sweater?

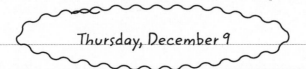

Thursday, December 9

My day would have been very different if Lula hadn't worn a striped sweater to school. But she did.

I sat at my desk and looked at the back of that sweater and thought, "I HAVE to fix one of the disasters in my life. I just HAVE to."

Then I tore a sheet of paper out of my notebook. And I wrote Lula a note.

I remember exactly what I wrote:

L—I am sorry I stole that piece of paper. I really, really am. I will NEVER do ANYTHING like that again. But can you please just PAUSE being mad at me? Because I NEED YOU. Remember how you didn't tell me about your dad because my family is so perfect? It is REALLY NOT! We have a crisis! I need your help! Will you PLEASE help me? —C

I leaned far forward and put my note on Lula's desk, but just like last time, she wouldn't open it. She turned and stuck it back on my desk.

That made me mad! She should at least read my apologies. It's the polite thing to do.

I put the note BACK on her desk. She stuck it right back on mine.

I picked up my pen. And in big letters on the outside of the note, I wrote, "CRISIS!! HELP!! PLEASE!"

I stuck it back on her desk. She waited this time. And read what I'd written on the outside. Then waited another few seconds. Then opened my note.

FINALLY, she wrote me back. This is her note:

FINE. Meet me in the bathroom.
Lula

One moment after I'd read that note, Lula raised
her hand and asked Mrs. McElhaney if she could
go to the bathroom. I waited a little bit. Then
I did the same thing. "I REALLY have to go," I
told Mrs. McElhaney. Some kids laughed at that
announcement. But I didn't care. I needed Mrs.
McElhaney to say yes, and she did, and I hurried
to meet Lula.

She was standing by the sinks, with her arms crossed.

"WHAT?" she said. Not at all nicely.

I glanced under the stall doors. To make sure no one
else would hear.

"It's Granny," I told her. "My crisis is Granny. And
it's the WORST."

I told her the whole story, from Granny forgetting
the word "shoe" to setting her sweater on fire.

By the end Lula had one hand over her mouth,

and she was almost crying.

"That IS the worst!" she said.

"I know," I said. "It's so rotten. And fighting with you is so rotten. Please don't make me do both. Please just be my friend."

"I won't make you do both," Lula said. "But don't read my notes anymore."

"I won't!" I said. "I promise!"

"Can I do anything else?" Lula asked. "For Granny?"

"I can't think of anything," I said. "Except—please don't tell anyone what's happening with her. I don't want anyone to know, except for you."

"I won't tell a single soul," she said. "I give you my solemn promise."

She held out her
hand, and
we shook on
it. Like we
always do,
when we give
each other
solemn promises.

I've never
actually thought
before about how
that feels. Shaking
Lula's hand
on a solemn
promise.

It feels really good.

But I had a hands PROBLEM later in the day.
Because in Spanish my nice friend Nora sent me
this note:

Celie,

Is Jo going out with Jake??
I just saw the two of them
by Jo's locker. They were
holding hands!

Your friend,
Nora

I couldn't BELIEVE Jo was holding hands with
Count Jake-ula.

Where the whole
world could see!
And when she
should've been
worrying about
Granny.

I had to go
see what was
happening. So
I told Señora

112

Santacruz I REALLY needed to go to the bathroom. Just like I'd told Mrs. McElhaney.

I guess Jack B. remembered. Because he said, "Celie rhymes with PEE-lie." Lots of kids started laughing, even though that joke is STUPID, and Señora Santacruz started saying things like, "¡Chicos! ¡Silencio! ¡Silencio!"

Then she told me I had to wait until she'd finished explaining the difference between two Spanish words that both mean "to be." It took FOREVER.

While she talked on and on, I grabbed my spy notebook from my backpack. And as soon as she nodded at me, I ran out the door with it.

I kind of forgot that I'm not supposed to spy on Jo.

She and Jake were still standing in front of her locker. I peeked at them from around the corner. Here is my spy report:

From the
Top-Secret Spy Notebook of
Celie Valentine Altman

Spies must at times take on a new identity. Try honing this skill as you spy.

<u>Who</u> are you pretending to be? Useful identities include, for example, janitors or cleaning ladies.

I cannot be the janitor. I'm ten.

What <u>props</u> are you using to improve your cover identity? A mop and bucket might be useful for cleaning employees, for example. But be wary of tools such as <u>vacuums,</u> which might impair your ability to hear your targets.

Okay. I won't vacuum.

Now that you are undercover, what do you <u>see?</u>

Jo is standing too close to Jake and holding

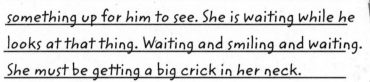

something up for him to see. She is waiting while he looks at that thing. Waiting and smiling and waiting. She must be getting a big crick in her neck.

Wait a minute! That thing she's holding up is her PHONE! She's not supposed to touch her phone during school!

And also, I'm pretty sure this is her lunch period! They should both be at lunch!

I had to run back to Spanish then. Because the bell rang. Everyone was leaving the classroom when I got back. "¡Chica!" Señora Santacruz said when she saw me. "Faster next time, you understand? ¡Rápido, rápido!" I nodded and waved.

Then I rápido rápido went to English. And hoped Jo wouldn't spend the whole entire day embarrassing herself.

A Little Later

What if your hands get all
sweaty when you're holding
hands with a boy? Or—
what if HIS do?

Yuck.

Later

Jo's phone keeps
buzzing with texts.
Text, text, text, text. I bet it's every girl in the
whole school, saying, "I saw you and Jake! I can't
believe you're going OUT! He's so TALL! Like a
basketball player! Do you have to stand on tiptoe
to whisper in his ear?" Or other ridiculous things
like that.

Unless it's a million texts from Jake.

I want to know who all the texts are from and what they say, but I can't ask Jo. Because that whole subject gets me in trouble.

So I left Jo and found an old frame in a living room drawer. Then I put the watercolor I'd painted for Granny in it, and I brought it to Granny.

"A spectacular painting from Spectacular Celie," she said, looking at it. "I have the perfect spot for it." Then she set it on her nightstand.

Now her nightstand looks like this:

I'm going to paint another picture of Granny, for myself. So my nightstand will look like this:

THAT is a good kind of hand-holding.

Later

Oh no. Oh no, oh no.

The phone rang a little while ago. Jo and I were reading in bed, and Dad's on a work trip. So Mom answered. I barely paid it any attention. But then Mom came into our room and closed the door.

Her face was very serious and very angry. And she was looking right at me.

I pushed my book away and sat up straighter and wished I could RUN. Because I was obviously in trouble.

"That was Violet's mother on the phone," she said.

"Violet's mother?" I said. And then I thought, VIOLET'S MOTHER? Because Violet's mother NEVER calls. Why would she be doing that now, and getting me in trouble?

"Yes, Violet's mother," Mom said. In the weirdly calm voice she uses sometimes before she explodes. "Apparently she has heard that Granny started a fire, in our kitchen. While you were baking with her. Is that true?"

My thoughts went crazy then. Because how did VIOLET'S MOTHER know about the fire? And what was I supposed to say to Mom?

Then, in a flash, I knew: Lula. Lula must have broken her promise and told Violet. And OF

COURSE goody-goody Violet told her mom.

"Celie?" my mom said. I'd forgotten she was waiting for me to talk. "DID Granny cause a fire while the two of you were baking?"

I still couldn't answer. Because I knew not to lie—Mom HATES lies. But if I told the truth, then Mom and Dad would worry about whether Granny might burn down the apartment. And maybe send her away.

Mom was raising her eyebrows at me and looking like her head might start spinning right off her neck.

Then Jo started talking. Trying, again, to save me.

I'd almost forgotten she was even in the room. She was sitting up in her bed, with her book pushed aside. Just like me.

"Don't be mad at Celie—you can't be," she said to

Mom. "She didn't want you to be upset with Granny and maybe send her off to some institution. That's TOTALLY understandable. She just loves Granny, that's the only reason she didn't tell you."

I wanted to crawl into bed with Jo then and hug her. I don't care if she holds sweaty hands with boys while she's supposed to be worrying about Granny. It was so nice, what she said.

But Mom had a different reaction. She said to Jo, "So you've known, too, this whole time." She sounded so disappointed.

"Yes," Jo said. In a much fainter voice.

"I need to hear exactly what happened," Mom said. "And I need to hear it right now."

So, finally, I told her exactly what happened.

By the time I'd finished, she just looked sad. She sat down beside me on my bed.

"I am so sorry you had to go through that," she said. "And I'm proud of how bravely and capably you acted in that moment. But I am NOT happy about what you did afterward."

She was quiet for a second. Then she shook her head and said, "I can't believe I encouraged you to bake. Things with Granny are changing so fast."

"You're not going to send her away, though. Right?" I said.

Mom started talking on and on then about how we have to work through all of this as a family, and she and Dad have a lot of decision-making to do that's going to have to happen sooner than they'd thought, and there's a lot of researching to do and processing to do together, and Jo and I had to PROMISE to tell her and Dad ANYTHING that raises any concerns AT ALL from now on.

I promised. Then I got a little distracted as she kept talking about family and responsibility. Because in

the back of my mind, I
was trying to figure out
WHAT I was going to
say to <u>LULA</u>.

I break
my solemn
promises.

Later

I can't sleep. I just walked past Mom's room on my
way to get a glass of water. Her door was closed, but
I could hear her voice. She must be on the phone
with Dad. I NEED to know what they're saying.

I thought about picking up the phone in the
kitchen VERY QUIETLY and listening in on
them. But what if I got caught? I'm in enough
trouble already.

So I didn't. I came back to my room instead. And
now I'm wide awake, worrying.

I'm thinking about Lula, too. Because first we're friends. Then we hate each other. Then we're friends. Then one of us is furious. Then we're better. Then the other one is furious.

I feel icky. Sitting here, thinking about it.

My friendship is making me sick.

Today did NOT turn out the way I thought it would.

Before our first class, I made Lula come with me to a quiet spot at the very end of the hallway. "I'm mad at you!" I told her. "Why did you tell Violet about the fire? You gave me your solemn promise!"

I expected her to get super-embarrassed then. I thought she'd turn blotchy and start biting her thumb. But that didn't happen at all.

Instead, she looked at me like I was CRAZY. And she said, "I DIDN'T tell Violet. I SWEAR. I didn't. REALLY."

She looked like she was telling the truth. But that didn't make any sense.

"You're the only person on the planet I told," I said. "And Violet's mom called my mom about it. How else could Violet's mom know?"

"I swear on the lives of Beijing and Shanghai," she said. "I did NOT tell Violet."

I had to believe her then. Because Beijing and Shanghai are our matching stuffed hippos. We only swear on their lives when we are very, very serious.

And then my brain put the pieces of the puzzle together.

"Ohhhh," I said slowly. And then I said to Lula, "Never mind."

"What do you mean?" she said. "What'd you just figure out?"

"I'll tell you later," I told her. "Sorry I blamed you."

I hurried to my desk then, because I knew the bell would ring soon. I wrote a note to Jo, as fast as I could. Here is what it said:

Jo—

I cannot BELIEVE you told Tall Jake our Granny secret. It's not like you're best friends with him! You've been on ONE DATE! ARE YOU GOING TO GIVE HIM MY DIARY, TOO?? WHICH YOU SHOULD NEVER EVEN BE TOUCHING?

—Celie

I rushed out of the classroom with that note and slid it into Jo's locker. Which made me thirty seconds late for math.

I wrote another note during Spanish, too. And I slipped it into her locker on my way to gym. It said:

Jo—

You have to stop holding hands with him. And talking to him. He obviously can't be trusted! Since I KNOW you told him not to tell anyone. And he went and told his MOTHER! So he's a goody-goody, too. Just like his sister.

—Celie

Later

Jo just got home. I asked her if she saw my notes.
She didn't answer. Instead she ripped a piece of
paper out of her notebook and wrote me this note,
while I was standing there:

Will you please just leave me alone now? I get your point.
Now please just leave me alone.

Jo

She's acting so weird! Writing that note instead of
talking to me. And not saying a word to me since.
She's not even answering her texts! She's just sitting
in a chair in the living room, looking out the window
and ignoring me. When her phone buzzes, she picks
it up and looks at it and then sets it back down.

"Don't you want to text back?" I asked a couple of
times. But she just kept looking out the window. As
if I wasn't there.

Her phone did ring once, and she answered it. She said, "Hey, Amber," in a flat voice, before she left the room. Then she stood in the hallway. I heard her say:

"I don't know."

and

"It wasn't good."

and

"I don't know."

and

"I DON'T KNOW!"

She didn't come back to her living room chair after that. I found her sitting on her bed, looking out the window.

It feels weird, following her around and watching her look out of windows. So silent. I wish she'd yell, "*NOBODY IN THIS WHOLE FAMILY UNDERSTANDS ME!*" and lock herself in the bathroom instead.

She's worrying me.

It's tiring to worry about Jo.

Later

Mom just went with Granny to run errands, so Jo and I are alone in the apartment. Mom's left us here without a grownup before, but not very often. And it always takes her a million years to get out the door. She keeps saying things like, "You're SURE you feel okay about this? You're SURE you don't want to come?"

When she finally left just now, I knew exactly what I wanted to do. I stopped thinking about Jo, still in her zombie condition in our room. I went to Mom's computer in the living room. And I started reading her emails.

I am NOT supposed to do that. But I needed to know whether she and Dad were making any plans to send Granny away. So I could prepare to fight.

I printed two emails out. Then I heard a noise and thought maybe Mom was back. So I grabbed those pages and ran out of the room.

This is a very scary one:

from: Pamela Trout <pamela.trout@youngatheart.com>
to: Elizabeth Altman <ealtman@xenithmail.com>
date: Friday, December 10, 12:48 PM
subject: Your request for information

Thank you for your interest in Among the Very Young at Heart Senior Home, where we provide only the finest in care for today's seniors. You can rest assured that your mother would receive all the assistance she could possibly need or desire here, from food, drink, and hygiene to medication management.

I'm happy to discuss rates and availability, as you have requested. Why don't we schedule a call so that I can learn more about your mother and her needs, and you can learn more about our facilities and services? What time works for you?

With all best wishes,

Pamela Trout
Senior Living Advisor, Among the Very Young at Heart Senior Home
Providing only the finest in care for today's seniors

That email is the worst thing ever written. I don't like Pamela Trout. We don't need her or anybody else giving Granny food and drink and medicine. WE can give Granny food and drink and medicine.

And what does she mean about HYGIENE? Is she going to put on Granny's deodorant? That's just disgusting.

Also, why is she a Senior Living Advisor? Do they have a Senior DYING Advisor?

I don't like that place. We are NOT sending Granny there. I will fight and fight about that. I will refuse to eat vegetables or brush my teeth. I will tell Mom I'm not covering the seat when I use public restrooms. (Even though secretly I actually will cover the seat. And brush my teeth. Because, yuck.)

Only, here's the confusing thing: Maybe I won't have to fight? Maybe Mom and Dad already agree with me? Because I also found this email:

from: Robert Carrion <rcarrion@grandprizerealty.com>
to: Elizabeth Altman <ealtman@xenithmail.com>
date: Friday, December 10, 3:12 PM
subject: Re: Listing 8601758, Riverside and West 157th

Elizabeth,

Yes, the listing is still available. I can personally vouch that it is a lovely 4-bedroom with loads of light, unusually deep closets, a cozy office space, and views clear to the Hudson. Well worth a look. And if I were in the market for an apartment right now, I'd be looking in Washington Heights, too. It's up-and-coming, with great subway access.

Let me know what times are good for you if you'd like to see the apartment, and I'll coordinate with the sellers.

Cheers,
Rob

Robert Carrion
Licensed Associate Broker
Grand Prize Realty
Member, New York City Top Realtors' Club

So, are we MOVING? To an apartment with four bedrooms? That is a lot of bedrooms! It must mean

Granny would stay. Why else would we need four? And maybe Jo and I would get our own rooms. My own dresser, without all of Jo's mess! My own door, so she could never lock me out!

But where is Washington Heights? I've never even heard of it. I'm worried that it's far.

I need to talk to Jo.

Later

TERRIBLE news about Washington Heights! It's VERY FAR!

Here's how I know: I told Jo the whole situation. At first she wasn't really listening to me. Because she was in her zombie condition. Even when I told her, "HELLO? This is an emergency!" she just said, "Go tell Mom."

"Mom's not even here," I said. "Remember? It's just the two of us."

That finally got her attention. Because she's supposed to be in charge when we're alone. She actually looked right at me for the first time since she got home.

"What happened?" she said.

I started telling her. She got more and more un-zombied. She was pretty sure her friend Crystal has a wacky aunt and uncle in Washington Heights. So we decided she'd text Crystal, to ask about it.

Jo promised she wouldn't tell Crystal WHY she was asking. Since we're not supposed to know that we might move there.

I got to look over Jo's shoulder while she was texting, to make sure she was keeping her promise. It was nice, sitting close to her and doing that. I miss it.

Anyway. The texts went like this:

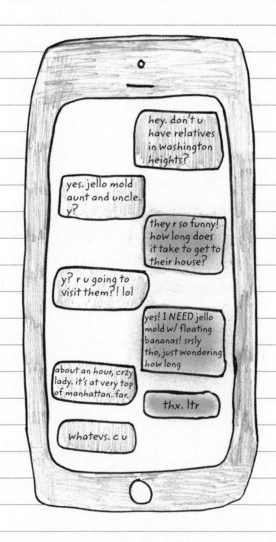

So Washington Heights is AN HOUR AWAY! Jo and
I are both freaking out! It's too far!

We can't spend an *hour* EACH WAY getting back and forth to school. Mom and Dad will definitely make us change schools. I'll never see Lula again! She's been my best friend MY WHOLE LIFE!

I'll miss other people, too. I'll definitely miss Nora. I'll even miss Jack B. and his stupid pee jokes. And the family that owns the bagel store down the street. They're all so nice. And what about Delores?? Can she travel that far? She HAS to keep cleaning our apartment. We love Delores.

What's wrong with a bigger apartment in THIS neighborhood?

Saturday, December 11

Jo and I found this invitation from Dad taped to our bedroom door when we woke up this morning:

Your mother and I hereby cordially invite you, our daughters, to

A FAMILY DINNER OUT

<u>When</u>: this very evening, 6 o'clock sharp

<u>Where</u>: Smokey Sadie's BBQ

<u>Dress</u>: Wear whatever you like. Only, please think twice before selecting those high-waisted jeans you've both taken to wearing. You tell me they're in style, and your mother tells me they're in style, but I wonder whether you all might have heard only part of the story. Could they in fact be in style <u>for grandmas</u>? Please consider.

<u>Speaking of Grandmas</u>: Granny will not join us tonight. She will be visiting with the one and only Cousin Carla.

<u>One final, vital note</u>: I am very sorry to have returned so late last night from a silly business trip, only to have to leave so early this morning for my silly office. Please know that the case I'm working on should quiet down soon. And never forget how much I love you both.

You haven't forgotten, right?

XOXOXOXOX,
Dad

Dad invites us to family dinners like this when we have important issues to discuss. So I guess we'll talk about moving and senior homes.

Poor Granny. Stuck with Crazy Cousin Carla, whose clothes are too tiny and who's always saying VERY INAPPROPRIATE things. Like telling me about her period! I would NOT want to spend that time with her.

Luckily, I've heard Granny say she thinks Cousin Carla is funny. So I'm hoping they'll have a good time.

Also, I'm glad Mom and Dad picked Smokey Sadie's. I love their pulled pork sandwiches.

Much Later

We're back. Here's a list of everything good and everything bad that happened at that dinner:

EVERYTHING GOOD

1. Mom told us that she and Dad have decided NOT to send Granny to a senior home. At least, not until they feel they have absolutely no other choice. I asked her, "Are you looking into it, though? Like, scheduling calls to discuss it?" Because I'm worried about her talking to Pamela Trout. "We're holding off for now," she said.

So that's very good. But it is the ONLY good thing that happened at that dinner.

EVERYTHING BAD

1. Mom and Dad think we have to hire a nurse to be with Granny for most of the day, almost every day. So a stranger will be in our house with us ALL THE TIME.

What if she chews with her mouth open? Or clips her toenails in front of us? Or sets the kitchen radio to classical music? Or stares and stares at me while I brush my teeth? I DON'T WANT A STRANGER IN MY HOUSE.

2. Our apartment is already too small. Having Stranger Nurse around all the time will make it feel even smaller. Even if Stranger Nurse is tiny. Which she won't be. She's not going to be a FAIRY. So we have to move.

3. Bigger apartments in our neighborhood are very expensive. We cannot afford a bigger apartment in our neighborhood. Not even if I stop buying clothes and only wear Jo's hand-me-downs and start selling my drawings online.

4. Bigger apartments in other neighborhoods like Washington Heights are not as expensive. So we have to move to another neighborhood. Maybe

Washington Heights. Maybe not.

5. Maybe we will have to change schools. Maybe not. Dad said, "It's early days yet. Let's not start pulling our hair out about that until we have to."

6. The pulled pork was too salty and the sandwich rolls were hard and dry. What has happened to Smokey Sadie's?

At least Granny and Cousin Carla were happy when we got home.

"She's teaching me hip-hop moves!" Granny told us when we walked in. She was sitting in a living room chair, and Cousin Carla was standing on the living room rug.

"Popping and locking, popping and locking," Cousin Carla said, jerking her body around.

She looked ridiculous! She's FORTY!

But Granny was laughing, and Cousin Carla was laughing, so the rest of us started laughing, too.

Cousin Carla,
Popping and Locking

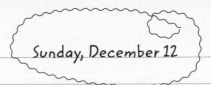

Sunday, December 12

We just got a weird call on our home phone.

When I picked up, a boy's voice said, "Um . . .
yeah . . ." With long pauses.

I thought it was a prank. I almost hung up.

But then he said, "Is Jo there?" And I was pretty
sure I recognized his voice.

"Is this JAKE?" I said.

He coughed and said, "Right." Then he said, "Hold
on a second." He muttered something to someone,
off the phone. I thought I heard "bad idea." Then I
heard a familiar voice in the background.

"Is that VIOLET?" I said. I definitely sounded
annoyed. Because she's ALWAYS around
somewhere, knowing things I don't!

Then Jake said, "Gotta go." And he hung up!

I went to find Jo. She was sitting at her desk doing homework.

I told her about the call. She got a little blushy. I could tell she liked that he'd called.

So I said, "Don't forget that he can't keep a secret." Because it's important for her to remember that! If he'd KEPT the secret, we wouldn't have to move and hire Stranger Nurse.

Jo got mad then and said, "I KNOW! I KNOW he broke his promise and got us into all this trouble— you don't have to keep telling me about it. But he's also a nice person, and it's not your business anyway. So just—STOP."

Then she swung away from me in her seat and started turning pages of her textbook, fast.

It's OBVIOUSLY my business. I thought about telling her that.

I also thought about saying, "He's way too tall for you, anyway."

But I didn't do either one. Because she was already shooting laser eyes at me.

Later

Jo and I should just be in separate bedrooms already. Because she keeps behaving like I'm not even here.

Angry Jo

Invisible Me

Today VIOLET got weird! She kept looking over her
shoulder at me during class, which she's never done
before. And her face was so CONCERNED.

I figured she was feeling sorry for me and my family.
Because she knows about Granny's mind.

You are not ALLOWED to worry about my granny, I
told her in my head. And I glared at her.

I wanted so badly to reach over and pull her hair,
hard.

I raised my hand instead and asked if I could go
to the water fountain. I used the word "parched."
Because Mrs. McElhaney always says yes when we
use words we've learned in class.

After I'd walked to the fountain, before I could
even push the button, VIOLET showed up.

"Did you FOLLOW me?" I asked her.

"I want to talk to you about something," she said.

You never want to talk to ME, I thought. You only ever want to talk to Lula. And if I move far away, you'll get to talk to Lula all the time, and I'll probably never even get to see her.

That thinking made me even MORE annoyed.

"This better not be about Granny," I said, in a not-nice voice. It definitely startled Violet. She didn't respond at all for a second.

"Granny is not your business," I told her. "You shouldn't even know about Granny."

"That's kind of what I wanted to say," she said. "Jake feels really bad about not keeping his promise to Jo."

"He SHOULD feel bad," I said.

"He was WORRIED," Violet said. "He thought

grownups should know about fires getting started."

"Why do YOU know?" I said. "You're not a grownup."

She ignored that whole point entirely and said, "He should've gotten Jo's permission before he told anyone—he knows that. He made a mistake."

"She wouldn't have given permission," I said.

"Like I said, he made a mistake," she said. "Haven't YOU ever made a mistake?"

She didn't actually pat the back pocket of her pants then, to remind me of my pickpocketing. But I still thought of those notes I'd stolen. And also, my stupid muttering of "Sky High Vi" in front of Lula. And reading Jo's texts when I wasn't supposed to. And throwing Granny's sweater down the chute instead of telling Mom or Dad.

"I told Jake to text Jo and apologize, and he did,

a bunch of times," Violet said. "But she hasn't accepted his apology. He tried calling her cell, too, but she didn't answer. So I got your home number for him, from the school directory. But then he got embarrassed when you answered, and he hung up."

"Huh," I said, feeling a little guilty. Thinking about how I'd told Jo to never trust him again.

"It's just, he was having a pretty bad year," Violet said. "Because our dad moved away over the summer. But then he started to like Jo, and Jo started to like him, and he was happier. Which was so good."

She paused for a second. Then she said, "I don't want him to be sad again."

I nodded. I don't like Jo being sad, either. Or a zombie. Or treating me like I'm invisible.

"I definitely can't control Jo," I told Violet. "But I'll try to help. I promise."

"Thanks," Violet said.

Then we both drank some water. And we headed back to class.

Later

I thought and thought about what to say to Jo when she came home from rehearsal. Finally I decided to draw her a picture. Here's a copy of what I drew:

At the bottom I wrote, "That's you and Jake, sitting in a tree. And it's fine with me. No K-I-S-S-I-N-G by your locker, though. Or anywhere else where anyone at all can see."

I waited by our front door and handed it to her the second she walked in.

She looked at it, then shook her head and told me, "You are so embarrassing." But she smiled a little when she said it. And she was at least talking to me!

It's not much to report to Violet. But I do think it counts as good news.

Later

I just called Violet on the phone. She liked my report. And we came up with a plan, to try to get Jo and Jake to school tomorrow morning at exactly the same time. So they'll have the perfect chance to make up.

I have to go tell Dad and Jo that we must leave for school tomorrow at PRECISELY 7:12 a.m. I'm going to lie and say I left an important worksheet in my locker and I know exactly how long it will take me to finish it.

I hope this works.

Violet and I are planning geniuses! She and Jake got to school exactly FIVE SECONDS before Jo and I did. I was actually ready to hug Violet when I saw her. That's how impressed I was with our brilliance.

We didn't hug, though. We just ran off together to the hallway near the lobby. I brought my spy notebook, so we could spy together. Here's my spy report:

From the
Top-Secret Spy Notebook of
Celie Valentine Altman

A spy uses equipment to carry out a successful mission. Numerous high-tech devices are readily available. Are you adequately prepared? List your equipment below.

What device are you using to help you <u>see</u>? Night goggles, for example, allow you to see in the dark.

We don't need night goggles. The lobby is very light.

We're peeking in there, at Jake and Jo, together. I'm trying to hear what they're saying.

What device are you using to help you <u>hear</u>? High-powered listening devices can be downloaded on many cell phones, for example.

I DO NOT HAVE A CELL PHONE!
IT IS ANNOYING TO ASSUME THAT
I DO!

Anyway, at this moment there is no need for a phone. Since Violet can ACTUALLY HEAR what Jo and Jake are saying! Her hearing is INCREDIBLE. She is a high-powered listening

device! Every spy should have a Violet.

I am writing down the conversation Supersonic Violet just heard:

Jake: "I'm really sorry. I messed up. I've been trying to tell you I'm sorry."

Jo: "I know."

Jake: "Hold on a second. I brought something for you."

Now Jake is digging through his backpack. Now he's handing Jo something.

Is that a coconut?

What device are you using to help you touch? Medical clamps (which resemble long scissors) might be useful, for example, to remove small objects from tight spaces.

I don't know a lot about medical clamps. But I'm
guessing they wouldn't work on a coconut.

Jo is holding the coconut just fine without medical
clamps. And she is grinning up at Jake.

I have to stop spying. Because WHY IS JO
HOLDING A COCONUT?

I asked Supersonic Violet why Jo was holding
a coconut.

"Jake wanted to get her something," Violet said. "As
an apology. When they went for ice cream, she said
she liked coconut as a topping. So he went to the
bodega around the corner from us and got her a
coconut."

"Okay," I said.

I wanted to say, "She meant SHREDDED coconut.
Just a little spoonful of it."

But I didn't. Because I would hate it if Violet made fun of Jo. And also, Jo wants me to be nicer about Jake.

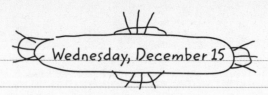
Wednesday, December 15

I haven't told anyone at school about The Move yet. Because so much is undecided. Maybe I'll stay at school. Maybe I won't. Maybe Mom and Dad won't find a place for a really long time. Maybe they'll find one tomorrow.

I don't want to hear questions when I don't have answers. It'd just make me worried. Plus it's hard to talk about WHY we're moving. Since it's hard to talk about Granny.

I haven't even told Lula. I was thinking I probably should. Today in math.

But then she tore a piece of paper out of her notebook and started to scribble on it. I thought she was writing ANOTHER note to Violet. I figured I was going to have to watch them AGAIN passing notes back and forth to each other. So I decided I'd never tell either one of them about the move.

Only, when Lula finished writing, she passed the

note to me! I passed it to Violet next. And we all three wrote together. Our notes are here, on this piece of paper:

Celie and Violet—Will you both spend the night with me at my dad's new place on Saturday? Please say yes. —Lula

Yes! Nothing could stop me.
—Celie

Me too! —Violet

Thanks. I didn't like thinking about being there alone. Not because it's a bad apartment—don't worry. The building has a gym, even, with spin bikes. —Lula

I understand about not wanting to be there alone. And also, I love spin bikes! The way they look, at least. I've never actually been on one.

—Soon-to-be-Spinning Celie

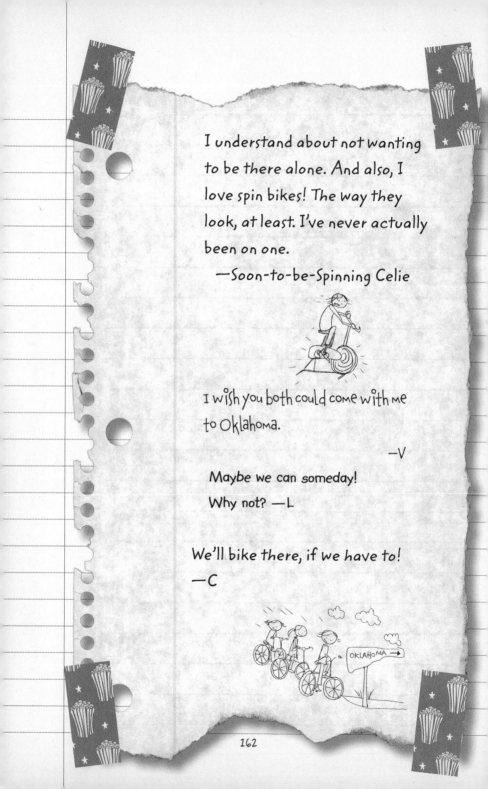

I wish you both could come with me to Oklahoma.

—V

Maybe we can someday!
Why not? —L

We'll bike there, if we have to!
—C

you're funny, celie! —V

Violet thinks I'm funny! And she and Lula and I are heading everywhere together! Why can't we be together in Washington Heights, too? Or wherever I end up.

It's like Granny says: Dark spirits lifting to light.

I'm writing really quickly, before breakfast. I don't want to forget what happened late last night.

I was wide awake, even though the lights had been out for a while. Jo was sleeping in her bed. I could hear her breathing in and out, in and out. And I realized something. My whole life, I've been listening to Jo breathe in and out, in and out, as she sleeps. If we get our own rooms, I won't hear it anymore.

Dad came to check on me and Jo then.

"What are you doing awake?" he asked quietly, when he saw that my eyes were open.

"I'm going to miss Jo's breathing," I told him, "if we get separate rooms."

He came and sat on the edge of my bed.

"We'll all miss things if we move," he said quietly. "But can we discuss NICE possible changes?

I, for example, have always dreamed of owning a pool table."

"We'd have space for a pool table?" I said.

"We might," he said. "Don't go crushing my dreams. You next."

I thought for a second about what I might like in a new place that was big enough for all of us to live together comfortably. With no mess. I thought about Lula and Violet visiting me there.

"I'd like three big beanbag chairs," I said. "And an old-timey popcorn maker."

"I think I can make that happen," Dad said.

"A cotton candy machine, too," I said. "Violet won't eat it, but Lula would."

"Hmm," Dad said. "I'm not sure we could fit a popcorn maker AND a cotton candy machine."

"They're smaller than a pool table!" I told him.

"An excellent point," he said. "Anything else?"

"Yes," I said. I had just that second come up with the perfect plan. "I dream of an art studio for Granny and me."

He leaned over and kissed my forehead then. "I love that dream," he said. "Let's work on that. In preparation, let's both get a good night's sleep."

He left the room after that. And I fell asleep to the thought of dreams coming true.

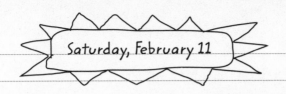
I just read back over this diary, and I CANNOT
BELIEVE how much has changed since I wrote it.
We moved ridiculously far from Lula and Violet, and
from our old apartment and neighborhood. Plus
right away we had to find a nurse to live with us. So
Granny could have all the help she
needed. It was hard finding
someone! We even had
to seriously consider
hiring a woman
with a pet bat.

I'm actually
very cuddly.

Thankfully that did not happen.

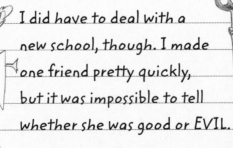

I did have to deal with a
new school, though. I made
one friend pretty quickly,
but it was impossible to tell
whether she was good or EVIL.

Also—and definitely worst of all—I did something bad. So bad that I got in way more trouble than I've ever been in. My parents practically put me in prison.

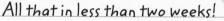

All that in less than two weeks! My hand was practically falling off by the time I'd written everything down. At least I made another friend who is 100% good. And we've gotten to eat lots of Granny's famous sour-cream coffee cake. That makes everything better.

Bye for now!

Here's a look at Celie's next adventure,

Everything's Changed

Do not even think about opening this journal. You don't get to read it. Or touch it.

It is PRIVATE.

You're not special just because you're my big sister, Jo. If you read this, I will find the picture I took when you had that giant pimple on your chin, and I will make copies, and I will tape them up in the hallway of our new school. Where everyone in your grade can see.

Don't assume
I won't do it.
Because I will.

Celie

Dearest Celie,

    I'm crossing my fingers that you'll like this
new diary. I went through shelf after shelf of
journals in the bookstore, trying to find just the
right one. I rejected a million (roughly speaking).
They seemed too businesslike, or too brown, or too
dainty, or too babyish, or too filled with supposedly
inspirational sayings like "Find the magic to make
your spirit fly."

    I found no such magic, but I did finally find
this journal. It strikes me as artistic and bold, and
those qualities remind me of you. So I bought it.

    I hope it feels like the right choice to you. And
I hope it helps you make your way through the days
we face ahead. I know it'll be hard to move to a
new home and a new school, and to have to worry
about making new friends. But changes aren't
<u>only</u> bad; they can be exciting, too. I know we'll
have happy moments as well as challenging ones,
and I hope it's helpful to you to describe them all
here.

With lots of love, and
then a whole lot more,

Mom

Once upon a time,

this diary became

the very

private

property

of

<u>Celie Valentine Altman</u>

And so it remains,

to this very day.

The End.